The House With No Name

by

Pippa Goodhart

Illustrated by Peter Kavanagh

You do not need to read this page - just get on with the book!

First published in 2000 in Great Britain by
Barrington Stoke Ltd
18 Walker St, Edinburgh, EH3 7LP

www.barringtonstoke.co.uk

This edition published in 2006

Reprinted 2007

ISBN 978-1-84299-377-4

Printed in Great Britain by Bell & Bain Ltd

MEET THE AUTHOR - PIPPA GOODHART

What is your favourite animal?
A dormouse
What is your favourite boy's name?
Mick
What is your favourite girl's name?
Tamla
What is your favourite food?
Fresh bread with butter and honey
What is your favourite music?
Mozart's Flute and Harp Concerto
What is your favourite hobby?
Mucking about with my family

MEET THE ILLUSTRATOR - PETER KAVANAGH

What is your favourite animal?
Grizzly bears
What is your favourite boy's name?
Poppa Bear
What is your favourite girl's name?
Momma Bear
What is your favourite food?
Porridge
What is your favourite music?
Let Me Be Your Teddy Bear
What is your favourite hobby?
Scratching

Contents

1 The House 1

2 Colin 15

3 Trouble 23

4 Dad 35

5 Camp Fire 41

6 Ghosts? 47

7 Exploding Free 61

8 Peace 69

Chapter 1
The House

"What's the house like? Is it nice?"
Jamie asked for the tenth time.

"You'll see soon enough," said Jamie's
Dad.

"But can I definitely have a bedroom to
myself?"

"A small one, yes. The girls will share
the biggest bedroom and Mum and I

1

will have the other."

Jamie folded his arms, relaxed back into his seat and watched the countryside passing by. It was usually Mum up here at the front of the van with Dad, Jamie and his sisters in the back. This time Mum and his sisters were at home and it was Jamie on the front seat.

He had the local map on his lap. The back of the van was full of tools and sleeping bags and food.

"So what *is* the house like? Mum reckons it must be falling down!" said Jamie.

"We got a local builder to have a look and he says it's fine. We've just got to patch the place up. It isn't even properly wired yet for electricity. We need to decorate and then it'll feel like home! Now watch out for a track on our left," Dad said.

They turned off the road onto a track running into the wood. The long branches of the trees on either side almost met overhead. The sunlight glittered through the summer leaves.

"This house is miles from anywhere!" exclaimed Jamie.

"You've got your bike," his father replied.

The trees hugged the track close on either side.

"It'll be dark at night," said Jamie. He was used to street lights. The thought of cycling down here with only the thin finger of light from his bike lamp to show him the way made him shiver.

Then the van bumped out of the tunnel of trees into a sunny clearing.

"There's our new home!" said Dad. "What do you think of it?"

****

It was the kind of house Jamie's sisters drew – a square with a door in the middle, a window at each corner and a sloping roof.

"It looks like a face!" said Jamie.

5

"Don't be daft!" laughed Dad as he took bags of tools from the van. "Now, have a quick explore and then come and help me carry this lot in."

The house did look like a face, a pale face with thatch for hair. The two upstairs windows glinted in the sunshine like winking eyes. The windows downstairs were boarded up with dark planks and looked like blushing cheeks. The faded red door was the mouth and the triangular porch roof above it was the nose.

Jamie ran from empty room to empty room in the house. It felt somehow alive. Jamie shook his head, puzzled, and went to join his Dad. A faint light leaked into the downstairs rooms through the boarded windows and showed a clean, old-fashioned kitchen.

Jamie's Dad waved a hand. He was looking around in surprise. "You'd never think there'd been an explosion in this room, would you?"

"An explosion?" Jamie asked.

"Yes. Ages ago. I heard that one person was killed." Then Dad snatched the baseball cap off Jamie's head and hung it over a nail on the back of the door.

"There," he said, "as my old Mum used to say, *when you've hung up your cap, you're at home.* So it's all yours now. Shall we have a camp fire tonight?"

"Yeah, great!"

"But first we've got to mend this window." Dad started knocking the boards from a broken window and tapping jagged bits of glass from the frame.

"When was this explosion?" asked Jamie.

"About 35 years ago, the man who showed me around said. A gas cylinder blew up. Faulty valve or something. The family who lived here left after that and the house has been empty ever since."

"Why didn't anybody else want it?"

"Well," said Dad, "houses are like people. They like company. So you find them mostly in groups in villages or towns. There's not many who like to be on their own."

Jamie grinned. "Now it's you talking about houses as if they were people. You said I was daft thinking the house looked like a face! Mum's the same. She told me this house needed cheering up with bright colours. *Cheering up* as if it had feelings!"

Dad smiled. "She's right, though. It does feel sad."

"Yes. Odd. Kind of frozen in time, waiting to be lived in again. But I like it."

"Good," said Dad. "Now go and fetch me a plank of wood to prop open the door, will you?"

As Jamie reached into the van, a cold shiver prickled down his spine. He felt he was being watched. He spun around to look.

Nothing moved except the leaves on the trees, stirred by a breath of wind.

Strange, he thought. He held the plank in front of him like a shield to protect himself as he hurried back into the house.

****

Jamie could forget about the creepy feeling of being watched, so long as he kept Dad talking.

"I've always wanted to live in a wood," said Dad.

"Why?" asked Jamie.

"We moved house a lot when I was little, always living in towns. I was forever moving schools and moving friends. I longed to settle in one place, in the country. So when Gran died and left us that money, I could do what I wanted at last, and I

found this place. And here we are," explained Dad.

"Why did you keep moving?" Jamie wanted to know. "Were Gran and Grandad on the run from the cops or something?"

Dad laughed. "What d'you think?"

Jamie remembered the photo of Gran and Grandad. He was small and sad and wore a flat cap. He remembered Gran's soft roundness and her iced cakes. They weren't crooks.

11

"They were on the run in a way," said Dad. "Running away from sadness rather than crime. I had a brother who died. Your Gran and Grandad thought the world of him."

"More than they thought of you?" asked Jamie.

Jamie's father paused. "They didn't want me to think that. They hardly even talked about him, but I always felt that he'd been more special to them in some way."

"Dad," began Jamie, "you know what you said about having to make new friends when you moved? Well, I've got to do that now, haven't I?"

"You can still keep in touch with your old mates," Dad promised him.

"But we haven't even got an address or a telephone yet!" Jamie objected.

"We'll soon sort that. What address would you like? Shall we call the house Woodside? Or Rose Cottage?"

"Boring," said Jamie. "It needs a special kind of name."

"For instance?"

"I'll think about it," said Jamie quietly.

Jamie and his Dad worked all morning, fixing new frames and glass into the kitchen windows. Again, Jamie felt that he was being watched. He kept glancing out of the window, hoping to catch a glimpse of whatever it was that was making his spine shiver. His ears ached with listening.

"Did you hear anything just then?" he asked his Dad.

"No," his father said, surprised.

Jamie's throat felt tighter and tighter. He was sure that somebody was watching him.

"I'll tell you this great joke, Dad," he said at last.

"Go on then."

"What has the bottom at its top?"

"Dunno. I give up."

Then a voice from outside said, "Easy! A leg has a bottom at its top!" There was a boy staring through the window, laughing at Jamie's shocked face.

Chapter 2
Colin

"Hello," said the boy. "Are you like the others who came and poked around or are you really going to move in?"

"Hi," said Dad. "Jamie and I are doing a few repairs before the rest of the family arrives. He was just wondering whether there might be any other lads living nearby. Are you from around here?"

"Yes," said the boy.

He wore a shirt like Jamie's PE shirt from school, narrow jeans and brown lace-up shoes. His red cheeks and shaggy brown-blond hair reminded Jamie of something or someone.

He wanted to ask the boy if they'd met somewhere before. He wanted to ask the boy if he had been watching them all morning, but all he said was, "Do you know any other jokes?"

The boy grinned. "What's black and white and black and white and black and white?"

"I don't know." Jamie shook his head.

"A penguin rolling down a hill!"

Jamie groaned. "All right then, what's this?" He bent the little finger on one hand and waggled it.

"A dancing worm?" guessed the boy.

"No! A microwave!"

"A what?" asked the boy, bewildered.

"Don't you get it? A microwave. You know, a very small wave!"

"Oh." The boy looked blank.

"Don't you have microwave ovens around here?" asked Jamie.

The boy shrugged his shoulders as if he didn't understand what Jamie was talking about. Perhaps things were old-fashioned in the country, thought Jamie.

His Dad winked at him. Then he smiled at them both. "I reckon I'll leave you two jokers to it and I'll fetch us all some lunch. I saw a fish and chip shop in the village." He then asked the boy, "Do you fancy joining us for lunch?"

The boy smiled. "Yes, please. I haven't had fish and chips for years and years and years!"

"What's your name?" asked Jamie as he began to sweep up the mess from the windows.

"Colin."

"How old are you?"

"Eleven. I should have been twelve soon."

"Should have been?" said Jamie. "Going to be, you mean. Same as me! I'll be twelve next week. Have you lived around here long?"

"Yes, years and years," said Colin.

"Who were those *others* you asked about. You know, the ones who only came to poke around?" Jamie asked him.

"They wanted to put a new house here. They were going to destroy this house to make room for it." Colin sounded angry.

"So why didn't they?" asked Jamie.

"They gave up and went."

"Oh." Jamie thought that Colin was a little strange, but he was friendly and the right age and a boy. Anyway, he was someone to do things with. "Which school are you at?" he asked. "I'm going to Claybrook Comprehensive next term."

"I've never heard of that one," said Colin. "I'm at Tetley Grammar School. I had to pass exams to get in. I wanted to be an astronaut. I needed to learn all I could about maths and physics. Don't you think it would be marvellous to land on the moon? They're planning to do that, you know!"

"They're not!" laughed Jamie. "They did that years ago! It's Mars they want to land on now. Do you really fancy being in space, thousands of miles from home?"

"Yes! You'd see the world from far away and you'd be free!"

"I think you're nuts!" said Jamie. "It'd be too lonely."

"It'd be beautiful. You'd see the world like a tiny ball in the sky."

"And the further you went the smaller Earth would shrink until it was just a dot and then it would disappear. Wouldn't that scare you?" asked Jamie.

"It'd be worth it, to escape," said Colin, sadly.

"Escape from what?" Jamie thought of his grandparents, forever moving but never finding peace. "You couldn't escape from your feelings. They'd go with you."

Chapter 3
Trouble

"Fish and chips are served," called Jamie's Dad as he stepped out of the van. He was carrying a steaming hot parcel in his hands.

Jamie was glad to see food and to have Dad back.

"Sit yourselves down on that log and we'll eat them out of the paper, the proper way."

Dad glanced at Colin. "Do you need to ring your Mum and tell her where you are?"

Colin shook his head. "Nobody'll miss me." He held a chip up in front of his face and ate it slowly, his eyes closing. "Mmmm!"

Jamie laughed, "It's only a chip, you know!" Then he turned to his Dad. "Guess what? Colin wants to be an astronaut!"

"Or a bird," said Colin. He pointed to a jay as it flew across the clearing and up into the sky. "I just want to be free to go, up into the open and away."

Colin knew all about the birds and animals and plants.

"Why don't you take Jamie into the wood and show him around?" suggested Dad. "I'll finish the windows. It'll be an early night tonight with torches and sleeping bags. My mate Gary's coming first thing tomorrow to help me wire the place up for electricity again. There's not much more we can do before then. You can paint those windows as soon as the putty's set, Jamie, but meanwhile, go and explore. Bring back some dry sticks for a camp fire. Are you going to join us for burnt sausages, Colin?"

"I'd like that," said Colin.

Colin led Jamie into the wood. Sunlight filtered through the leaves.

"I'll show you where to find fir cones for the fire. They're really good for getting the fire going because they're oily."

The wood all looked very much alike to Jamie, lots of trees and bracken and paths that seemed to head off in every possible direction.

"I'd soon get lost in here," he said.

So Colin showed him how to work out where he was by checking the position of the sun in the sky. Then he showed Jamie the different plants and birds, pointing out footprints and nibbled stems and scratched bark left by different animals.

"And look at these!" said Colin. "D'you know what these are?"

"Yes, I do know. Nettles!" said Jamie, but Colin was pointing to something on one leaf.

"See that? Butterfly eggs. Just hatching."

"Blimey! The caterpillars are tiny!"

"Sometimes I feel like a caterpillar," said Colin. "Just existing and staying where I've been left. I wish I could cocoon myself into a chrysalis and come out as a butterfly."

"You do say some weird things," said Jamie.

"Have you ever watched a butterfly coming out of a chrysalis?" asked Colin.

Jamie shook his head.

"I have. They come out all crumpled and squashed. They look as if they'd never be able to fly. But the sun warms them and their juices push into the veins in the wings. This makes them stretch out wide and flat like kites. Then the butterfly flaps his wings and he's off to get nectar from flowers instead of munching nettle leaves." Colin sighed.

"So you really do want to fly?" asked Jamie.

"More than anything. I want to go, up and away and be free," said Colin. "See that?" He pointed to a massive clump of tall flowers growing in a patch of light between the trees. "It's called rosebay willow herb, but I call it the rocket plant. See?" He pointed to the tall stems of bright pink flowers pointing up towards the sky like rockets on a launch pad. "Aren't they brilliant?"

Jamie looked at Colin to see if he was kidding. None of his friends at his old home would have admitted to liking flowers,

especially pink ones, but Colin was serious. And he was right. The flowers were lovely.

"Who's that?" asked Jamie as something laughed in the trees.

"Only a woodpecker," said Colin. "Don't you know any bird noises? They do have birds in town, don't they?"

"Yes," replied Jamie, "pigeons and sparrows. And I know what cuckoos sound like."

"I hate cuckoos," said Colin. "They lay their eggs in little birds' nests. When the cuckoo chick hatches, it pushes out the little birds' chicks. The poor mother bird has to feed the blooming great cuckoo chick, even when it gets bigger than her. Her real babies just die."

Colin picked up a stick and began swishing it through the bracken and bramble undergrowth.

Then he said, "I called my little brother Cuckoo. He was adopted."

"I've only got sisters," said Jamie.

"Cuckoo was a baby when he came to us. Mum and Dad thought he was wonderful. He took up all of Mum's and Dad's time so there was none left for me."

"Didn't you like him at all?"

"Oh, yeah! He grew and I taught him things – how to swing himself, that kind of thing. I loved him. And I hated him. You know."

Jamie laughed. "I know."

Then Colin suddenly looked intently at Jamie. "Have you ever hated somebody – really, really hated them – just for a second? And you've told them you hate them and even ... even told them that you wished they were dead?"

Jamie nodded. "Yes. You can hate what somebody does, but still love them. It gets mixed up."

"That's it! That's what happened to me," shouted Colin.

"How d'you mean?" asked Jamie.

Colin pointed to an old log. "See the marks on that?"

Jamie could see marks scratched into the log.

"There's a C curling around a T," Colin told him. "Those initials are mine and my brother's. I let my brother use a knife to make his T. He was too little and he cut himself." Colin paused. "I think I killed him."

"You what?" Jamie felt suddenly cold.

"I think I killed my brother."

"*Did* you kill your brother?" asked Jamie.

"I think so." Colin threw his stick. "I don't know!"

"Then go home and find out!" said Jamie. "I bet he's fine! Have you run away because of that?"

Colin just traced a finger over the C and the T in the wood. Jamie noticed that the marks seemed old.

"Look, if you're in trouble, you can stay with us tonight," said Jamie. "Dad'll sort it all out. He's got his mobile with him."

Again, Colin looked puzzled but said nothing. He gave a brief, stiff smile.

They collected firewood in silence, but as they headed back to the house, Colin suddenly shouted and dropped his sticks. He clutched at his head.

"What's up?" asked Jamie. Colin held his hands out in front of himself and stared at them in horror. His fingers held a small bunch of hair. "Blimey!" said Jamie. "How did that happen?"

With a wild cry Colin turned and ran towards the house. What was wrong? Was he feeling ill?

Jamie remembered that there had been a boy at school who'd had cancer and his hair had fallen out when he was having treatment. It grew back afterwards.

I'll tell Colin that, thought Jamie. But a sudden shout and a terrible crashing noise made Jamie forget that and run.

"Dad!"

Chapter 4
Dad

An empty ladder leaned against the house. Colin stood below it, hands pressed to his mouth as if he was trying to hold in a scream.

On the ground lay Jamie's Dad.

"Dad! What happened? Where are you hurt?" Jamie's hands hovered over his Dad, frightened to touch him.

Dad opened his eyes, but his forehead was damp with sweat and he was shaking.

"Leg," he said, pointing downwards. Then he closed his eyes again as the pain hit him.

"Don't move!" Jamie told him. "You might have hurt your back or something."

Dad's right leg was bent in a way that a leg shouldn't be able to bend. "Colin, go and find a telephone and ring for an ambulance. Quick!"

Colin ran off, and Jamie turned back to his father. "What happened?"

"I was up the ladder, just pulling out a bit of thatch from the roof to see what condition it was in. Then something kind of blew me backwards off the ladder."

"Was it Colin? Did he do it?"

"Don't be daft, Jamie. No! Colin came running from the wood as I fell, but he wasn't near when it happened. He was shocked, poor lad. When I saw his face I thought I must've died!"

"You could've ..."

"I know, Jamie. But I didn't and I won't. It's just my leg that's bad. You'll have to get in touch with your Mum and go back home for now."

Jamie held his father's hand and stroked it, and talked about how they'd turn the house into the best home ever. Then, at last, the ambulance came rocking up the track with Colin running behind.

The ambulance people loaded Dad onto a stretcher, wrapped him in blankets, strapped him down, and lifted him into the ambulance.

"Will he be all right?" asked Jamie.

"He'll be fine, but what about you?" asked the ambulance man.

"I'm going to phone my Mum and go back home."

"Good boy." They closed the ambulance doors and drove off slowly over the bumpy track.

As he watched it grow smaller in the distance, Jamie felt horribly empty. "Show me where the phone box is, Colin. I've got to ring my Mum. I suppose she'll go to see Dad at the hospital. My sisters and me'll be dumped on my Auntie Sheila."

"Why not stay here?" asked Colin.

"On my own?" Jamie sounded shocked.

"I'll be here," Colin promised him.

"I wonder if Mum would let me? I could paint those windows to surprise Dad. And I can help Gary with the wiring tomorrow."

So Jamie telephoned home and asked Mum if he could stay with a friend. He didn't actually lie, but he knew that his Mum thought he would be staying at Colin's house with his family.

She asked, "Has Dad met this Colin?"

"Yes. He likes him," Jamie assured her.

"All right, then. I'll be over to pick you up tomorrow. What's this boy's address?"

"Don't worry about that, Mum. I'll be at our house when you arrive."

"OK, love. Take care. Bye!"

Chapter 5
Camp Fire

"Have you really run away?" Jamie asked Colin. "I've sometimes thought about doing that."

Colin shrugged. "I'm not where I should be."

Jamie smiled, "So I'm going to spend a night in a haunted house with a runaway!"

"Why d'you say haunted?" asked Colin.

"Somebody told my Mum it was."

"You don't seem bothered about it."

"I'm not." Now, with Colin here, the place didn't seem spooky.

"Let's light the fire," said Colin.

"Good idea. The matches and frying pan are in the van. Dad brought fire lighters and bread and ketchup and drinks and things. I think he even remembered a tin opener for the beans."

Colin knew about making camp fires. "I was in the Scouts," he told Jamie.

The shadows of the evening stretched out longer. First flames licked around the sticks. Then they grew strong. They spat through the damp wood and at last became roaring hot.

"Hungry?" asked Jamie.

"Starving!" said Colin. "I've not had a sausage for years and years!"

"You've not done anything for years and years according to you!" said Jamie. "Dad was looking forward to bonfire sausages."

Colin looked up to where the ladder still leaned against the roof. "You told me he wasn't going to hurt the house, but he was pulling it to bits!"

"Only looking at a tiny bit of thatch. What's wrong with that?"

Colin was staring up at the roof and fingering his head. He's turning strange again, thought Jamie.

He told Colin, "You butter the bread and I'll open the beans."

They ate as the wood and house darkened around them. As the firelight died to a faint glow, Jamie said, "Give us the torch and I'll get the sleeping bags from the van."

Chapter 6
Ghosts?

They laid the sleeping bags on the floor of the front bedroom, using cushions for pillows. Without washing or changing into pyjamas, they wriggled into the bags.

Jamie told Colin, "Your wish has come true. You're a caterpillar cocooned in a chrysalis!"

When they lay quietly, Jamie could hear noises all around. The house creaked slightly and its pipes hummed. The wind breathed in and out of the chimney hole in the bedroom.

A sudden yipping, screaming sound came from outside, making Jamie gasp.

"Only a fox," said Colin. "Sometimes they sound like a small boy screaming."

"It's all right," said Jamie. "I didn't think it was a ghost or anything. I don't believe about the house being haunted."

Colin didn't respond, so Jamie asked, "Do you believe in ghosts?"

"Yes."

"Really?!" Jamie wanted to see the expression on Colin's face. He switched on his torch. Its beam lit up Colin lying there in

Dad's sleeping bag. Colin blinked into the light.

"I know that you don't believe," said Colin. "But that doesn't matter. It doesn't stop the ghosts from believing in you."

"Oh, ha ha! Are you trying to scare me?"

"No."

Jamie sat up in his sleeping bag and waved his torch beam around the room. "This is my laser sword!" he said. "I can zap all ghosts and ghouls with its deadly power!"

"What's a laser?" asked Colin.

"You know! Those long straight lights that can cut. Like surgeons use! Like the ones they fight with in *Star Wars!*"

Jamie beamed the torch light right into Colin's face again, making him put up his hands to protect himself. His pale skin seemed almost transparent.

"Blimey, you really look as if you've seen a ghost!" said Jamie.

"I have. Lots of times."

"What, here?" asked Jamie.

"Yes," replied Colin.

"Really?" There was no hint of a teasing grin on Colin's face. Jamie's throat felt suddenly thick, but he managed to laugh. "What's it like then, this ghost? How old?"

"About our age," said Colin.

"No! I mean, how old in history. Does it clank about in armour or a long dress or what? Does it go moaning about the place saying 'Wooooooo!' and walking through walls?"

"No."

"Then what? What does its face look like?" Jamie insisted.

"I don't know. I haven't seen that bit."

"Is it a headless ghost?" Jamie sliced a hand across his throat.

"No." Colin looked at Jamie. "If you like, I'll tell you about it."

"Go on, then," whispered Jamie.

****

Jamie settled himself, propped on his elbows. Colin breathed in some of the darkness of the old house, and began.

"There was once a man and woman who loved each other. They lived in this house in the woods and they wanted children."

"Is this a fairy story?" asked Jamie.

"D'you want to hear it, or not?"

52

"Yeah. Go on."

"Well, they had a baby boy. It grew up and went to school and did all the usual things like have measles and learn to swim and go fishing. Then the man and woman wanted another baby, but no other baby came. After nine years, they asked the boy if he would like them to adopt a brother or sister for him. The boy knew what his Mum and Dad wanted him to say, so he said *yes*. So the baby came."

"Boy or girl?"

"Another boy. He grabbed the first boy's toys and cried all night and Mum and Dad were always busy with him. There was never time for fishing trips any more. Mum was always feeding the baby or cleaning him or playing with him and Dad was always working hard to pay for the extra things they needed. So the bigger boy felt pushed out."

"Was the baby called Cuckoo?" asked Jamie.

"Yes." Colin's face was paper pale. "The one I killed."

"By a little knife cut accident?!"

"No. It wasn't then. I killed him later, and it wasn't an accident. It was a time I really meant to hurt him, but I didn't really mean to kill him." Colin's eyes were wide with pain.

Jamie put a hand on the hump that was Colin in his sleeping bag cocoon.

"How did it happen?" he asked.

"Cuckoo was four years old. One day he went into my room and he took this model I'd made of the rocket they were going to send to the moon. He took it downstairs and he got Mum's rolling pin and hit and hit and hit it until it was smashed to bits. When I found what he'd done, I wanted to smash him."

"I would've too," offered Jamie, but Colin wasn't listening. His eyes were fixed on this scene from the past.

"Cuckoo was out on the swing under the ash tree. The sun was shining on his black hair and he was all happy and smiling proudly because he'd just learnt to swing himself. He saw me and he shouted for me to look how high he could go. He didn't even realise that the smashed rocket mattered. I wanted so badly to hurt him, to make him cry like I was crying."

"You're crying now."

"It was easy to kill him." Colin laughed a short, unfunny laugh. "I just shouted his name, and waved."

"Waved?"

"Yes. With both hands." Colin blotted his eyes with a sleeved arm and focused on Jamie once more. "You see, we had a game where I would do something – stick out a tongue or hop on one leg or something – and he'd copy it back. And this time he copied my two-handed wave and that made him fall off the swing."

"Then what happened?"

"I watched him fall. I enjoyed him falling. Then he landed on the ground and screamed, and the next moment my hate exploded and we were all dead."

"Hate doesn't explode!" A sudden thought stabbed into Jamie like an icicle. As it melted a cold shudder went through him. "When was this, Colin?"

"I killed Cuckoo in 1965."

"Dad told me that a gas cylinder exploded here in 1965. One person died, but I don't think ..."

Colin put his hands over his ears. "No! Don't tell me! I can't bear it!" He was shaking. "That's why I stopped everything stone still when my hate exploded! I won't go on and see what happened! I can't! I've kept it the same here for years and years and years, keeping it how it was ..."

"You frightened away the developers?"

"Yes!" said Colin fiercely.

"Was it you that made my Dad fall off the ladder?" gasped Jamie.

"I don't know, Jamie. Maybe! I didn't mean to, but I'm bad. I do kill things. Your Dad was pulling out my hair when he was pulling out the thatch. It hurt and I shouted for him to stop, but I never touched him!"

Colin's eyes were deeply sad. Jamie wanted to turn away, but Colin touched his arm. "I think I can kill people without touching them, Jamie. I did that to Cuckoo and to my Mum and Dad. And now your Dad."

"My Dad's not dead, Colin."

Suddenly something that had been puzzling Jamie made sense. "You said that Dad was pulling your hair?"

"Yes. Pulling out great clumps of it."

Very quietly Jamie asked, "Colin, is this house you?"

Colin nodded. "Yes. That's how I've kept it like it was. The house is me. And I am the ghost."

Chapter 7
Exploding Free

What Colin had said still didn't all make sense. Jamie told him, "My Dad said that only one person died in the explosion. And it was a faulty gas cylinder, not hate, that exploded."

"I was there," said Colin. "I know what happened. My hate burst out and killed Terry and my parents."

"Who?" Jamie sat up. "What name did you say, Colin?"

"Terry."

"Is that Cuckoo's real name?"

"Yes."

"My Dad's called Terry!"

"So what?"

Jamie wriggled out of his bag and crouched beside Colin. "Listen, Colin, my Dad was adopted too. Was your Terry dark-haired like my Dad? Is your surname Hall?"

Colin sat up and his eyes showed that the answer was yes.

"Then my Dad must be your brother!" shouted Jamie. "He must be! He's alive and his Mum and Dad were alive until not long ago. They were all alive except you, Colin. My Gran – your Mum – only died last year. You were the only one killed in the explosion."

The house suddenly juddered and lurched as if it was being shaken by a small earthquake.

Jamie jumped up from his sleeping bag and stumbled to the window. In the first light of morning, the world outside looked grey. Out in the yard, a small boy swung back and forth under the big ash tree.

A sudden shaft of light shone through the window. It shone right through Colin so that Jamie could see the sleeping bag and floorboards through his friend.

Colin cast no shadow on the floor.

Jamie looked at Colin's smiling face, saw him pull himself free of the sleeping bag cocoon.

"Colin?" Jamie reached out a hand to touch Colin's shoulder, but his hand went straight through. "Don't go, Colin. Look through the window. It's happening again. There's Cuckoo!"

The small, dark-haired boy on the swing was tipping back and forth to work himself higher.

"Watch," Jamie told Colin. "Let it happen this time. You'll see he'll be OK."

It was like watching a silent film. The boy on the swing looked towards the house and shouted. His mouth was open, but there was no sound. He laughed, then he lifted his hands from the swing ropes to wave, and he fell. His mouth was scream-shaped.

"Quick!" Jamie was running down the stairs, dragging open the door and running out to the small child who was his own father. Two other figures were already by the child as the little boy sat up, fists to eyes. Six arms, the man's, the woman's and Jamie's, reached for the child and at that same moment a massive noise boomed through Jamie's body, hurling him to the ground.

For a moment Jamie lay, stunned, his mind so shaken by the noise that he couldn't think. But as his thoughts settled, he knew what the sound was that rumbled and tumbled behind him, even before he looked.

"Colin!" he shouted. "Colin, your Mum and Dad didn't die. You saved them! You made Terry fall and that made them run outside and miss being caught in the explosion. You didn't kill anybody, Colin. You didn't! You saved them all, and they loved you always!"

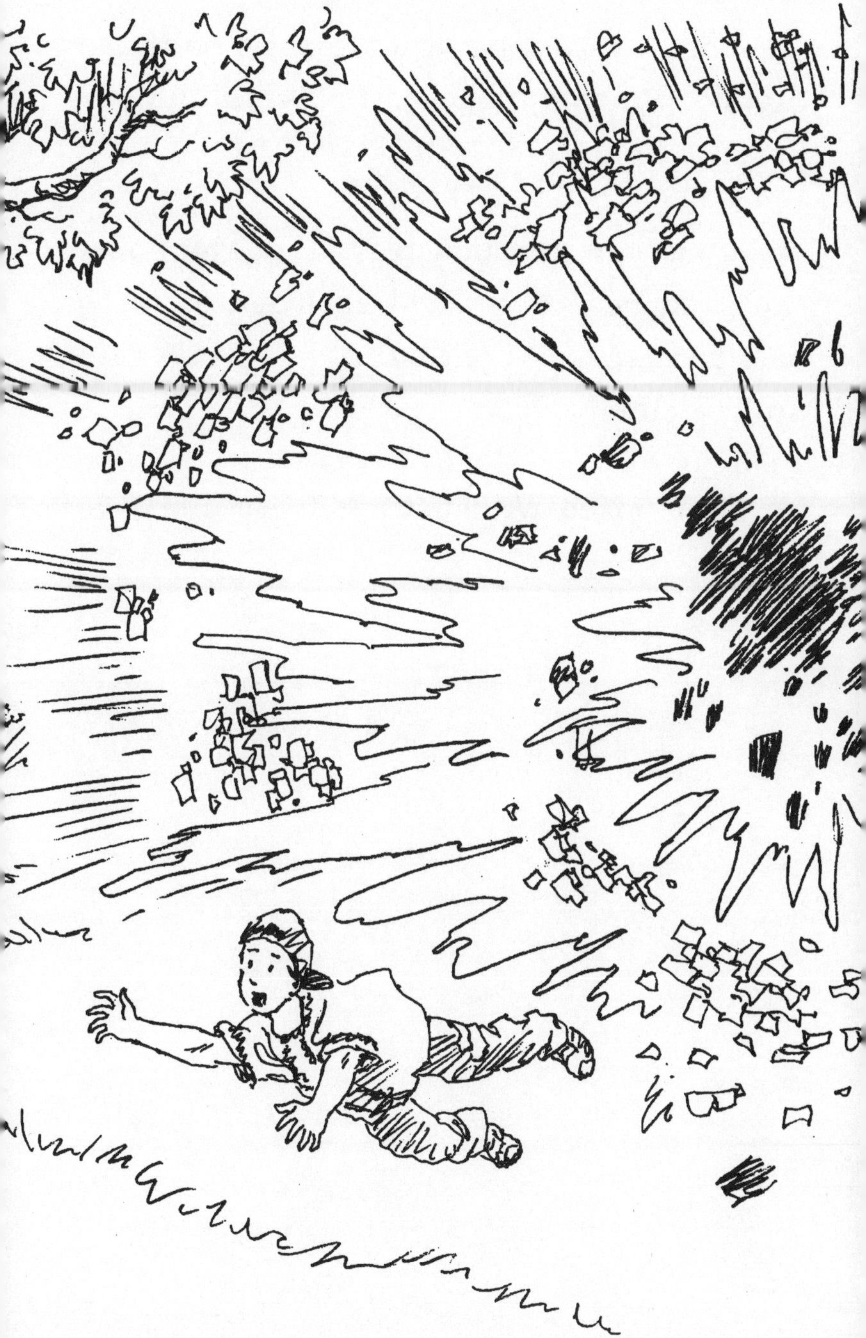

Jamie pulled himself up to kneel on the ground. He was alone. Little Terry and his parents had gone.

Jamie saw through tears that the house that had been Colin had exploded. Colin was free. It was exciting. It was beautiful and terrible.

Jamie cried with both sadness and joy.

Chapter 8

Peace

Jamie sat, stunned. He watched the sun rise and the house sigh and settle to rubble. Dust rose like steam and glittered in the morning light. Now and again the rubble shifted into a more comfortable position. The roaring, crumbling, rumbling collapse was over. The house was at peace, and the main sound now was cheerful birdsong.

"Are you free now, Colin?" Jamie asked the air.

The place felt calm, and the place was Colin. Sunlight fell where it hadn't for years. The shadow cast by the house was gone, and so too was the sense of sadness.

Jamie wiped a sleeve across his damp eyes and got up. Then he ran through the early

morning wood to the place where the rosebay
willow herb grew.

He reached down and pulled at the long
stems with their great rocket cones of pink
flowers. He pulled and pulled until his
hands were sore and his arms full of the
flowering stems.

He carried the flowers back to the house
that had been Colin. He clambered over the
crumbled ruin, sure that nothing would
injure him because the house was his
friend.

He climbed to the place where the
fireplace and part of the chimney still stood
among the rubble. He thrust the rocket
plants into the broken chimney hole as if it
were a vase.

Then he stood looking up into the sky and
thought of birds and butterflies and people. He

thought of space rockets.

"Goodbye Colin," he said. "I'll tell Dad –
tell Cuckoo – about you. We'll make a new
house and live here always."

And Jamie knew that Colin would be in the
birds and flowers and stars that surrounded
their new home.

He would be a part of this place forever.

Barrington Stoke would like to thank all its readers for commenting on the manuscript before publication and in particular:

Patrick Bonner
Martin Burns
Philip Costello
Laura Dillon
Lianne Hughes
Cheryl Kirk
Katie Mackay
Patrick McIlhalton
Damien McMullen
Robert Nisbet
Lauren O'Keefe
Elena Soper
Gary Thompson

Become a Consultant!

Would you like to give us feedback on our titles before they are published? Contact us at the email address or website below – we'd love to hear from you!

E-mail: info@barringtonstoke.co.uk
Website: www.barringtonstoke.co.uk

If you loved this book,
why don't you try ...

Zack Black and the Magic Dads

by Annie Dalton

Zack doesn't think he needs a dad, but his mum thinks he does. The Magic Dad website seems like the perfect way to make her happy ...

But it's not that easy. With each new Magic Dad, things go from bad, to worse to crazy!

Can Zack find a new dad – or is he looking in all the wrong places?

You can order *Zack Black and the Magic Dads* from our website at www.barringtonstoke.co.uk